D0943199

BUGS BUNNY

SEE SYLVESTER'S
AMAZING JUGGLING ACT

Flip the pages rapidly and watch the pictures in upper right-hand corner as the characters seem to come alive!

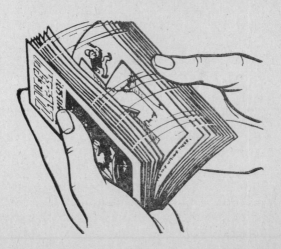

BUGS BUNNY

THE LAST CRUSADER

by

Rita Ritchie

A WHITMAN BOOK

Western Publishing Company, Inc.

Racine, Wisconsin

© 1975 Warner Bros. Inc.
All rights reserved.

Produced in U.S.A. by
Western Publishing Company, Inc.

WHITMAN and BIG LITTLE BOOK
are registered trademarks of
Western Publishing Company, Inc.

No part of this book may be reproduced
or copied in any form without written
permission from the publisher.

CONTENTS

Enjoying the Scenery

CHAPTER 1

HAUNTED CASTLE

The tour bus chugged through the desert in the country of Isitsand. Inside, Bugs Bunny wiped his brow. "Whew, it's hot! Where is this ruined castle we're going to see, anyway?"

Sylvester said, "Hey, what's the hurry? Enjoy the scenery." He aimed his new movie camera out the window and started filming. "F'r instance, there's a picturesque camel caravan over yonder sand dunes."

"You're a real filmin' fool, doc," marveled Bugs. He looked at all the camera equipment in the luggage rack. "Hundreds of feet of the airport, the Isitsand capitol, and every village we've gone through, not to mention miles of sand dunes."

"You ought to take it up, Bugs," said Sylvester. "It's a fine hobby."

At last the bus stopped near the

"You're a Filmin' Fool."

crumbled walls of an ancient castle. Everyone got out and stood in the shade of some palm trees.

The tour director said, "You are the first group to visit this recently discovered castle of the Crusader period. Everything is remarkably preserved. The local natives stay away from this place because—heh-heh—they believe the ruins are haunted. But several motion picture companies have already expressed interest in using this castle as a movie set. Step this way."

"Hurry up, Sylvester," urged

A Crusader's Castle

Bugs. "We'll be left behind."

Sylvester stopped filming, and they entered the castle after the other tourists. The big courtyard was empty except for one man. "Say, doc, where's the rest of the crowd?" asked Bugs.

"They went into the main hall," the man told him.

But when Bugs and Sylvester crossed the courtyard, they found several huge doors. "Which door do we take, doc?" Bugs called over his shoulder. "Doc? Hey, Sylvester, the guy's disappeared!"

"Where's the Crowd?"

"Poking around in some odd corner, no doubt," said Sylvester. "Listen. I hear voices."

Following the voices, Bugs and Sylvester soon caught up with the tour. The director pointed at some wall hangings. "Note the tapestry pictures showing everyday life in Crusader times."

"Must get movies of that," said Sylvester. Stepping back, he began filming.

The crowd followed the tour director to another corner of the hall. "See the weapons, arranged in neat

Admiring an Old Tapestry

rows, as if ready for the Crusaders' hands," he pointed out.

Sylvester spoke to a tourist standing near him. "Excuse me, sir —would you step aside so I can film those swords?"

"Certainly," said the man.

Sylvester filmed the old weapons for several seconds, then turned back to the tourist. "Much obliged, sir— Hey! Where'd that guy go?"

Bugs hurried over. "What's the matter, Sylvester?"

Sylvester explained that the man he had just talked to had vanished.

"Where'd That Fella Go?"

"Bugs, they say this old castle is haunted. Y'don't suppose—"

"Aw, don't let your imagination run away! This place is creepy, all right, but any ghosts dried up and blew away hundreds of years ago."

"Nonetheless, Bugs, let's stay close together," said Sylvester. "I wouldn't want *you* to disappear."

They kept close to the crowd until the tour director finished his lecture. Then the man said, "Now you have a chance to examine this wonderful old castle by yourselves. Please be sure to meet back at the

"This Place Is Creepy!"

bus in half an hour."

"Look, Bugs," Sylvester whispered. "A man's going down that corridor alone. Let's see if he disappears the way the other two did."

"Waste of time," muttered Bugs. But they followed the man as he walked down the corridor, looked at some tapestries, and then entered one of the castle's rooms.

When Bugs and Sylvester reached the room, it was empty!

"Where'd he go?" wondered Bugs. "There's no other door and no furniture but an old table and a

Empty!

couple of benches."

Sylvester searched behind some suits of armor. "Not here, either."

"There must be a trapdoor," said Bugs. "If he fell through, nobody would know but us. Look hard!"

As they started probing among the floor stones, there came a rumbling sound. Suddenly a section of the floor dropped from beneath their feet.

"Yipes!" gasped Bugs. He and Sylvester plunged down into darkness. "Oof!" Bugs landed on something soft. "YEOWP!" he cried as

"Yipes!"

Sylvester crashed on top of him. "Hey, that camera stuff's got sharp corners!"

Sylvester lit a match. "Luckily, this pile of tapestries kept things from breaking. Where are we?"

"In some cellar, I guess," said Bugs. "Here, light this old torch I found." When it was burning, Bugs held it high. "Hmm ... our man isn't here, Sylvester."

"Guess he found a way out. Let's get going, friend!"

With Bugs lighting the way, they walked along long, dark tunnels.

A Long, Dark Tunnel

Once in a while they passed doorways to empty rooms. "Must've been dungeons," said Bugs. "Look! There's a light straight ahead!"

They hurried to the light and found themselves at the bottom of a winding stairway. Bugs put out the torch. "Going up, doc! Second-hand armor on three, used tapestries on four." Bugs scampered up the stairs.

Sylvester followed. "Say, Bugs, don't you hear voices somewhere?"

"Must be the tour. Maybe they're boarding the bus. Step on it, chum!"

Scampering up the Stairs

Bugs ran up the stairs, which wound around and around. "Where's the end to this, anyway?"

WHAM! Bugs crashed into something cold and hard.

Blinking away stars, he found himself at the top of the stairs, staring up at a man in helmet and chain mail, his gauntleted hands resting on the hilt of a huge sword.

"I-I don't believe it!" Bugs stuttered. "B-But it's a Crusader—and he's real!"

"It's a *Real* Crusader!"

CHAPTER 2

SIR ROGER'S VOLUNTEERS

As Bugs stared at the armored Crusader, Sylvester called up the tower stairway, "Bugs, wait for me!"

"Down, doc, down!" cried Bugs. He leaped to his feet and immediately tripped over the Crusader's outthrust foot. CRASH! Birds

A Quick Trip

chirped in his aching head.

Sylvester reached the top of the stairway. "Zounds!" the cat yelped, seeing the Crusader. "It's a solid ghost!"

"Run, chum," said Bugs weakly.

"W-We'll f-face the apparition t-together, B-Bugs," said Sylvester, his camera gear rattling as he shivered and shook.

The ghostly Crusader spoke. "There is no escape. Look behind you!"

Coming upstairs behind Sylvester were three more armored men.

"There Is No Escape!"

They barred the way with big spears.

"Here are two more men for you, Sir Roger," said the first knight.

"Very good, Sir Ed," replied Sir Roger. "I've got all the best prospects now. Wait here while I go down and scare off those snoopers." He clanked down the tower stairs.

Bugs got to his feet. "Sir Ed looks familiar, Sylvester. Didn't we see him in the castle courtyard?"

Sylvester peered closely. "Sufferin' succotash, Bugs, you're right! And this other guy—"

Sir Roger Leaves

"Sir Don," said the second knight.

"And I'm Sir Max," said the third.

"You're the three tourists who disappeared!" exclaimed Bugs. "What's up, doc?"

"That's for Sir Roger to explain when he comes back," replied Sir Ed in a firm voice.

Distantly they heard the echo of ghostly laughter, followed by screams. Bugs felt the hair stand up on his neck. "Listen, you three! Let's get together and tackle Sir Rocks-in-the-Head when he comes

"You're the Three Tourists!"

walking up those stairs."

"No, no!" said Sir Max. "You'll ruin everything!" He sidled up close and whispered, "They're making a movie, get it? And we've all been picked to act in it."

"Er . . . and who told you this, buddy?" asked Sylvester.

"I figured it out myself," said Sir Max. "Remember what the guide said about their wanting to make movies here? They're trying to see how well we can improvise."

Chains rattled far below, and more tourists yelled in fright.

"You'll Ruin Everything!"

"Let's improvise an escape," suggested Sylvester, setting off at a run. But there was no way out of the round tower room.

Sir Don came over to them. "Don't try to run away. This is just a rehearsal for a historic movie."

"Is that so, doc?" asked Bugs. "History of what?"

Sir Don shrugged. "Something from the Crusader period. Maybe a battle. I figure they picked us to find out how well we can play along with it. Golly, just think: me, in a real Hollywood movie!"

"Don't Try to Run Away."

When Sir Don walked away, Sylvester said, "Blimey! Wonder what the third chap thinks."

"Forget it," said Bugs. "I see a way out of this batty belfry." He led Sylvester to one of the open slit windows. When nobody was looking, Bugs quickly tossed out the end of a long hanging curtain. "We'll both climb down to the parapet below."

Sylvester looked worried. "Suppose there's no parapet below?"

"Has to be, doc," said Bugs. "This whole joint's full of ledges, walls,

Bugs Has a Plan

roofs, and stuff. See you later, chum!"

Bugs leaped through the window and grabbed the trailing curtain. *Rip!* The old fabric began to tear. Bugs looked down at a hundred feet of empty space. "Help!"

"Coming, Bugs!" Sylvester dived out the window.

"No, no!" yelled Bugs. "Back, back!"

Too late. Sylvester grabbed the torn drapery. *R-i-i-ppp!*

"Yipe!" Sylvester cried. The two of them swung at the end of the

Hanging On

badly frayed curtain.

The heads of the three knights appeared at the window. "Don't move!" ordered Sir Ed. "We'll get a rope."

"Hoo-hoo-haw-haw!" echoed the laughter of Sir Roger.

"Th-this is no laughing matter," whimpered Sylvester.

"He's trying to scare the tourists," said Bugs. The curtain ripped a little more, and he gulped. "D-Don't breathe s-so hard!"

The three knights dropped a rope out the window. Bugs and Sylvester

Tossing a Rope

grabbed hold and were pulled up.

"Whew! Am I glad to see you guys!" sighed Bugs in relief.

Sir Ed leaned close. "If you keep this up, you won't get any prizes."

"I sure don't win any in the brain department today," Bugs admitted.

"I mean from 'Sneaky Cinema,' " whispered Sir Ed. "You know, the TV show with a hidden camera. They see how people react to situations they set up for laughs. You get prizes if you play it cool. I'm sure we're on 'Sneaky Cinema.' "

Sir Roger came clanking upstairs

"You Won't Get Any Prizes!"

to the tower room. "Ha! Those med-
dlers took some scaring, but they
finally ran off when you men
shrieked."

"That was us, doc," said Bugs.

"Splendid!" cried Sir Roger.
"What presence of mind! You two
will make a worthy addition to my
army. Of course, you will join, won't
you?"

Bugs glanced out the window at
the tour bus roaring away into the
distance over desert sands.

"I guess now we'll have to, doc,"
he answered.

The Bus Roars Away

CHAPTER 3

THE ARMY MARCHES

Sir Roger led Bugs and Sylvester to a room containing a dozen suits of armor. Weapons and shields hung on the walls. "Put on this chain mail," he said to Bugs. "And this suit should fit Sylvester."

Soon Bugs and Sylvester were each outfitted like a Crusader.

Knightly Outfits

"Hark to yon enemy!" cried Sylvester, flourishing his sword.

"This castle's pretty well hidden by cliffs, doc," Bugs said to Sir Roger. "How'd you find it?"

"I have always lived here," said the Crusader.

"Always?" repeated Bugs disbelievingly. "Just cute little you and nobody else?"

Sir Roger frowned. "My earliest memory is of waking up with a terrible headache years and years ago."

"I'd get a headache, too, stuck

Sylvester Swings His Sword

out here in Nowheresville," Bugs agreed. "Sure must've been lonesome."

"My ancestors kept me company," said Sir Roger, waving a hand at the tapestry pictures of knights and ladies hanging on the walls.

Bugs gulped, remembering that the castle was supposed to be haunted.

Sir Roger said, "Enough tarrying! We must set out at once."

"Er . . . where're we headed for, sir?" asked Sylvester as the Crusader quickly marched them down

Clanking Down the Stairs

the narrow tower stairs.

"There is a river a few miles away, which I have seen from the highest tower," Sir Roger said. "My army marches toward it today."

The other three knights were waiting in the castle courtyard. "Sir Roger, we have wild goat's milk in skin bags and sacks of dates ready for the march," reported Sir Max.

"Could you maybe dig up a carrot or two?" Bugs asked hopefully.

"Kneel down!" Sir Roger commanded. Then he touched Bugs on

Ready for the March

the shoulder with his sword. "I dub thee 'Sir Bugs.' Hmm . . . that's not a very knightly name, is it?"

"I'll have you know I come from a long line of nightly kinfolk, doc," Bugs retorted indignantly.

Sir Roger knighted Sylvester and then lined up his army. "Forward!"

Sir Don carried the flag, and the others came after him with supplies. Sylvester staggered along with a sack.

"Sack too heavy, doc?" asked Bugs.

"I've got my camera gear under

"I Dub Thee 'Sir Bugs.'"

my armor, Bugs," Sylvester said. "Camera, film, developer—"

"Don't let Sir Iron Britches see the stuff," Bugs advised. "They didn't have cameras seven hundred years ago, and I have a funny hunch our moonlit knight would break up the set."

"You think the old boy's cracked?"

"He's no ghost," said Bugs. "And I can't figure out why a real somebody would go through all this, unless he ran away from a funny farm and never returned."

"He's No Ghost."

For several hours, the crusading army marched up and down hills and across burning desert. The sacks got lighter as they ate their rations. Finally they reached the river.

"Oh, boy!" cried Bugs, running forward and jumping up in a high dive. "Me for a bath!"

Splash! Bugs sank like a stone in his heavy armor.

"Hold your breath, Bugs!" yelled Sylvester, quickly shedding his armor and hiding his camera gear under it. He dived into the water

Sylvester to the Rescue

and, following a trail of bubbles, found Bugs and dragged him up. The other knights pulled them to the bank.

Sir Roger frowned. "It's not the river we want to capture, Sir Bugs. Just one of the boats on it."

"One's coming now," said Sir Ed.

"Quick! Up that tree!" commanded Sir Roger. They scrambled into a tree whose branches hung far out over the river. Sylvester, having stopped to put on his armor, was the last one up.

A fishing boat drifted silently

Preparing an Ambush

toward them, its lateen sail flapping lazily. When the deck was beneath them, Sir Roger hissed, "Sir Bugs, lead the attack."

"Wh-who, me?" Bugs clung desperately to the branch.

Sir Roger picked up Bugs in one big fist and Sylvester in the other. He dropped them onto the deck of the fishing boat.

"*Aiee!*" cried the fishermen. "Ghosts of the ancient warriors have invaded our boat!"

"Unlax, fellas," said Bugs. "We're friends." He ducked suddenly as a

Dropping In

fisherman lunged at him with an oar.

"Charge!" cried Sir Roger. He and the other three knights jumped aboard.

Grabbing oars and boathooks, the fishermen fought against Crusader pikes and broadswords. Sylvester skipped around the deck, inches ahead of a pronged fishing spear held by an angry native. "Help me, Bugs!"

Lowering his helmeted head, Bugs pounded across the deck and butted the man into the river.

Bugs Uses His Head

"Better watch out, Sylvester," he warned. "These boys are playing for real!"

"I still can't bring myself to hurt 'em, Bugs," Sylvester said.

"Neither can I," said Bugs. Glancing around, he added, "Nor can our three knightly dupes. Only Sir Roger's really fighting, and he's a goner if all the sailors gang up on him. C'mon, it's up to us to handle this so nobody gets hurt!"

Grabbing a halyard, Bugs swung across the deck into the back of a native who was menacing Sir Ed.

Swinging Into Action

Splash! The fisherman went into the river.

Bugs tipped over some barrels and rolled them down the tilting deck, upsetting the other natives. One barrel split open, spilling its contents on the deck.

"Fish!" cried Sylvester.

As he leaned over to pick up a sturgeon, somebody poked him with a boathook. "YEOWP! Unfriendly fellow!" Sylvester smacked him with the fish. The other grabbed a large sturgeon and hit Sylvester right back.

Rolling Out the Barrel

Bugs was quick to take advantage. Breaking open more barrels, he ran among the Crusaders, pushing fish into their arms. "Load up for a full-scale battle, men!"

Soon each side was flailing the other with fish. Bugs skipped here and there, pushing off-balance natives into the river.

The last two fishermen scooped up sharp knives from the deck. "Run the invaders off the boat!" cried one.

The Crusaders nervously clutched their fish, while Sir Roger

A Full-Scale Battle

called, "Ho, where is my sword?"

Bugs ducked behind the boom, where it slanted down to the deck. As the two desperate men began their rush, Bugs pushed. The boom swung across, sweeping the men into the river. They quickly swam ashore and ran after their fleeing companions.

"Victory is ours!" cried out Sir Roger. "Tomorrow we set sail to conquer this land!"

While the three knights cheered, Bugs went looking for Sylvester.

He found him down in the hold,

"Victory Is Ours!"

lying, with swollen stomach, among piles of fish bones.

"*Urp!*" said Sylvester . " 'Scuse me, old buddy. Just takin' a small lunch break."

Taking a Lunch Break

CHAPTER 4

A-CONQUERING
WE WILL GO

The next morning, after breakfast, Sir Roger assembled his army
on deck. "We're going to sail down-
stream, capturing every river village along the way," he told them.

"Why the sweat, doc?" asked
Bugs.

"But how else can we establish a

"Why the Sweat, Doc?"

kingdom in Isitsand?" asked Sir Roger. "After all, Sir Bugs, there are other things in life besides goat's milk and dates, and I mean to have them."

"You mean things like riches and castles and serfs?"

"Yes, exactly as the old tapestries showed me. What other way is there for a full-grown warrior to earn a living?" He raised his sword high. "Up with the sail! On with the conquest!"

They sailed down the river for a long time before sighting a village.

"On With the Conquest!"

"Get ready to attack!" ordered Sir Roger.

"Psst, Sylvester! Stop shaking!" said Bugs. "Your armor's rattling."

"Th-that's my c-camera and film c-cans, Bugs," said Sylvester. "They're under m-my armor."

When the boat reached the village, Sir Don swung the sail over, and Sir Max threw a line around a palm tree.

"Charge!" cried Sir Roger as he and his men leaped to the bank.

Bugs and Sylvester clambered off the boat and stood behind some

"Charge!"

huge jars, watching the other Crusaders running to the houses. Natives yelled in fright and dashed away.

"Er . . . care to partake of a battle?" asked Sylvester.

"No, thanks. I bruise easily," said Bugs. "Besides, when the villagers get over being scared, they'll see that they outnumber us tin-can soldiers."

"Duck! Sir Roger's looking our way!" warned Sylvester. He and Bugs crowded behind the big jars. "I say, mate, quit pushing."

"Quit Pushing!"

"Shove over, will ya?" demanded Bugs. "Hey, l-look out!"

One of the big jars toppled over and smashed open. Gallons and gallons of olive oil gushed out. Slipping and stumbling in the oil, Bugs and Sylvester crashed into more jars. A river of olive oil ran down the village street, sweeping Bugs and Sylvester along.

"Yoicks, tallyho!" cried Sir Sylvester, brandishing his sword.

They rode the slippery river past their astonished fellow knights. Natives saw the uplifted weapons

"Yoicks, Tallyho!"

speeding toward them and ran for their lives.

"Look out for that curve," Bugs warned. "It's a lulu!" They *swooshed* around the bend, banked off a convenient house, and squirted away down another street.

One or two villagers threw stones, but, as the coasting Crusaders zoomed nearer, they lost their nerve and joined the other villagers, who were running to the distant hills.

Bugs and Sylvester swooped toward a wall at the far end of the

Coasting Crusaders

now abandoned village.

"Last stop!" called Bugs, nimbly leaping atop the wall as the oily stream splashed to a halt.

Sylvester skidded to a stop. "Great sport, Bugs. Shall we go it again?"

"Splendid!" cried Sir Roger, running up to them. "What zeal! What eagerness for battle! But, Sir Bugs, don't let the enemy escape next time. We need them for serfs."

They loaded some captured goats and food supplies into their boat. Then they set off down the river

Skidding to a Stop

for another conquest.

When they came to another village, Sir Roger said to Bugs and Sylvester, "You shall have the honor of leading the charge. Now, remember, we want to capture subjects for my kingdom."

"Yessir, your knightship!" Bugs saluted. "Okay, Sylvester, let's go!"

They leaped over the side of the boat and ran down the village street, followed by the other knights.

"Hey, Ahmed!" yelled a small boy. "Look at the crazy suits they're

"Let's Go!"

wearing! They're all metal!"

"Ithn't that hot, mithter?" lisped
a little girl.

"Bugs, this place has nothing but
small fry!" exclaimed Sylvester as
curious children crowded around
the armored knights.

"Our parents all went to sell their
sheep," explained one boy.

Sir Roger looked disappointed.
"This isn't much of a conquest, but
it'll have to do. Children, we're Crusaders, and we've just captured
you. Get aboard the boat at once!"

"What'th a Cruthader?" lisped

"Children, You've Been Captured."

the small girl near Sir Roger.

An old woman hobbled toward them, cackling with laughter. "Crusaders, eh? The children are too young, and I'm too old, to be scared. Now, get!"

Sir Roger turned red with anger. "Old woman, you're my prisoner!"

"Sic 'em, kids," ordered the old woman.

A stone bonged off Bugs's helmet, and his head rang like a bell. The sweet-looking little girl sank her teeth into Sylvester's tail, sending him up high in the air with a yell.

"Sic 'Em, Kids."

Suddenly the street filled with swatting sticks and flying rocks.

"Swords! Shields!" yelled Sir Roger, fending off blows. "Attack!"

A clay water pot crashed over Sir Don's helmet. Bugs got tangled in a bolt of cloth, and when the old woman yanked the end, he whirled off giddily down the street. Sylvester ran past with a wooden pail jammed over his head.

Then the embattled knights heard a terrific pounding noise. "Camels!" yelled Sir Ed, pointing. "The kids stampeded 'em at us!"

Embattled Knights

The mean-tempered beasts galloped through the streets, and the invading army turned and ran.

"*Yeouch!*" cried Sir Roger as a camel nipped him from behind.

When they reached their boat, the knights quickly cast off and sailed away. Gloomily, they patched their armor and bandaged their wounds.

Sir Roger spoke through gritted teeth: "We won't give the next village a chance to strike back!"

Bunny brains, help me out! thought Bugs. Then he snapped his

Mean-tempered Camels

fingers. "Sylvester, we've got to get out of this mess. Listen. . . ."

Sylvester nodded in agreement as Bugs unfolded his plan.

When the next village came into sight, Bugs and Sylvester jumped off the moving boat.

"Wait!" cried Sir Roger. "We're not there yet!"

"Meet ya on Main Street, doc!" Bugs replied.

Running along behind rocks and bushes, Bugs and Sylvester reached the back of the village unseen. Hiding behind the last house, Bugs

Bugs Tells His Plan

pulled out a fishnet he had hidden under his armor and unrolled it across the village street.

"We let the first crowd run over the net," Bugs reminded Sylvester. "They'll be the villagers, running away. The next bunch'll be our canned crackpots. We pull the net tight for them."

"I hear 'em coming now, Bugs!" warned Sylvester.

Bugs and Sylvester ducked out of sight as the sound of yells and running feet grew louder and closer. A crowd dashed over the net in a blur.

Unrolling a Net

Hard on its heels, the second group came charging.

"Pull!" cried Bugs. The net sprang taut. *Whang-o!* People pitched and squirmed in the meshes. "Now, wrap 'em up!" said Bugs. Quickly he and Sylvester tied the net tightly closed.

"Excellent!" said Sir Roger from behind. "You've captured them all!"

"Huh?" Bugs looked around at the Crusaders. In the net, struggling, were the men, women, and children of the village. "But who—"

"Pull!"

Bugs began to ask.

Sylvester pointed. "Goats, Bugs! That first group was the village's herd of goats."

Sir Roger sheathed his sword. "After we seize everything of value, we'll put these slaves to work."

"Why not stop for lunch first, doc?" suggested Bugs.

"We haven't eaten since morning," Sir Max added.

Sir Roger agreed. Leaving the captives snug in the net, the Crusaders took food from the houses and sat down to eat it in the shade

Lunchtime

along the riverbank.

"Oops, we forgot the lemonade," said Bugs. "Let's see if we can find a jarful, Sylvester."

As soon as they were out of sight, Bugs started running. "Quick! We'll turn the villagers loose, and then they can help us overcome Sir Roger!"

"Better think of something else, mate," said Sylvester, slowing down a bit. "The captives have vanished."

Bugs looked in dismay at the pieces of fishnet lying in the street.

An Empty Net

"They cut themselves loose!"

Far out in the desert rose a cloud of dust, stirred up by the fleeing villagers.

Fleeing Villagers

CHAPTER 5

ESCAPE BY SAIL

"My first prisoners—gone!" sighed Sir Roger. "This crusading business isn't as easy as I thought."

Bugs patted him on the shoulder. "Cheer up, doc. You can always go into the fishing trade."

"Impossible!" cried Sir Roger. "I come from a family of conquerors.

"Cheer Up, Doc."

We'll load the boat with loot and then sail on!"

They added cheese, dates, and half a dozen horses to their booty before setting sail.

Late that afternoon, they sailed into a huge lake. Sir Roger ordered the boat anchored. "We'll make camp on shore tonight."

The knightly crew took the six horses and the supplies ashore.

"Tomorrow," said Sir Roger, "we'll start building a fortress here. Then I'll have a place to keep all

Unloading the Horses

the prisoners we capture from the villages around the lake."

The knights groaned at the idea of so much work.

"How long will the construction take, my lord?" asked Sylvester.

Sir Roger yawned and stretched. "Two or three months." He sat down with his back against a big rock. "Now you two can . . . make supper . . . while I. . . ." In a moment, he was snoring. The other three knights were already asleep.

"Quick, Sylvester!" said Bugs. "Now's our chance to scram. We

"Let's Scram!"

have plenty of daylight left for sailing that boat."

"Bugs, y'don't mean to sail back upstream, do you?" Sylvester asked. "We left behind some terribly angry villagers. They would probably ambush our boat."

"Yeah, they sure would. But there must be plenty of villages around this big lake." Bugs started hauling up the anchor. "We'll get a bunch of locals to grab our sleeping beauties until we can get everything straightened out. Pull up the sail, will ya?"

Preparing to Sail

Bugs headed the boat out into the lake. Soon they were clipping along under a brisk evening breeze.

"*Ulp!* Sufferin' succotash!" said Sylvester in disgust. "Bugs, we left in such a hurry, I forgot to take my camera stuff along. It's back with the supplies we unloaded for Sir Roger. Uh ... y'don't suppose you could—"

"Sorry, chum. Nothing doing," said Bugs. "We'll rescue the stuff when we net Sir Crackpot and his three slightly chipped vessels— er—vassals."

"I Forgot My Camera!"

Soon Sylvester spied a village on the distant shore. Bugs headed the boat toward it.

On the shore, a boy was watering a herd of sheep. Bugs called out to him, "Hey, sonny, go tell—"

"*Aiee!*" cried the boy. He ran back to the village, sheep galloping all around him. "Help! The armored invaders!"

"Gee, I forgot we were still wearing armor," said Bugs, tying up the boat.

As they entered the village, people ran in all directions, shouting,

"Help! The Armored Invaders!"

"The Crusaders are coming!"

"Word of Sir Roger's activities sure did spread fast, partner," said Sylvester.

An old man shook his fist at them. "We're prepared for you raiders." He yelled over his shoulder, "Quick, man the palm tree!"

"Hey, wait!" Bugs called out. "We're friends. No swords, can't you see?"

"Fact is," added Sylvester, "we've come to ask for help."

FLOOP! A nearby palm tree whipped wildly in the still air.

"Wait! We're Friends!"

ZOOM! A huge rock skimmed low over Sylvester's head.

Another palm tree was being bent far back.

"Uh-oh—I get it!" said Bugs. "They're making catapults out of those palms. Clever, these Isitsandians!" CRASH! The next rock landed right in front of them.

"Back to the boat, pal!" cried Bugs, racing down the street.

He and Sylvester scrambled aboard and pulled up the anchor. "We'll talk to them after we back off a little into the lake," said Bugs.

"Back to the Boat!"

ZOOM! Another rock shot past, barely missing the mast.

"They're in no visiting mood, Bugs," said Sylvester. "Let us betake ourselves to safer parts."

Bugs swung the tiller over. "Okay. We'll soon be out of their range."

SMASH! The next rock broke through the hull. Water gurgled in swiftly, and the wood boat began sinking.

On the shore, the villagers cheered. The boat drifted out of their range.

A Direct Hit

"There's just time to make a raft before we sink," said Bugs. "Lucky it isn't dark yet."

Bugs and Sylvester swiftly assembled a raft. The sun had set by the time they pushed off from the sinking boat and began paddling.

"Where to, pal?" asked Sylvester, peering into the dark. "I can't see a blasted thing."

"Me neither," Bugs admitted. "But we'll keep paddling till we find the shore. It may take hours."

They paddled their raft all through the night. When the moon

"We'll Keep Paddling."

rose, they could see nothing but inky water. They took turns sleeping. At last the dawn broke.

Bugs sighed wearily. "There's the shore, not too far away, Sylvester. We must've been paddling mostly in circles."

They turned the raft and headed straight for land. An hour's hard paddling brought them to a stretch of lonely beach. They staggered ashore and flexed their stiff limbs.

Sylvester sniffed eagerly. "Food cooking nearby, Bugs! Perhaps we could beg a bit of breakfast, eh?"

Sylvester Smells Food

Bugs quickly agreed. They followed their noses along the beach and around a cliff. Four armored men crouched beside a fire.

"Oh, no!" moaned Bugs.

It was too late for him and Sylvester to duck back out of sight.

Sir Roger stood up. "Where did you go?" he demanded. "We've been looking all over for you two!"

"Where Did You Go?"

CHAPTER 6

A FORT FOR CRUSADERS

"It's like this, Sir Boss," Bugs said as Sir Roger scowled. "While Your Knightships were sleeping, my buddy and I sailed to another village. They must've heard of you, because they had rigged a catapult. They sank the boat. Sylvester and I made it back on a raft."

Bugs Explains

Sir Roger raised a big mailed hand and brought it down heavily on Bugs's shoulder. "What courage! To take on a whole village, just the two of you! Never mind the boat. I saw a great fort some distance away. We'll march inland and take it by storm. That's easier than building one."

"It—gulp!—is?" asked Bugs.

After breakfast, they saddled the horses and loaded supplies. Sylvester hid his camera equipment among his other gear.

"Let's take a gander at this fort,"

"What Courage!"

Bugs suggested. They scrambled up a rock pinnacle atop a nearby cliff. "Yipe!" cried Bugs, staring.

Far away, miles across the desert, rose several towers made of steel girders.

"Fort, my foot!" said Sylvester. "Bugs, those are oil derricks!"

Bugs nodded. "And the 'fort defenders' are apt to put up a mean fight. Scaring villagers is one thing, but tackling an oil field is pretty serious stuff."

"What're our chances of fading out of sight?" asked Sylvester.

Oil Derricks

Sir Roger roared from below, "Sir Bugs! Sir Sylvester! Come down at once!" He waved his sword impatiently.

"Offhand, I'd say our chances are kinda slim," Bugs replied.

Led by Sir Roger, the Crusaders rode for hours across the desert.

"Say, doc," Bugs called out, "how far away d'ya figure this fort is?"

"We should reach it in two or three days," said Sir Roger. Then suddenly he ordered, "Halt!" and reined in his horse.

"Halt!"

"What's wrong?" asked Sir Ed.

"There is a great serpent lying in the sand beyond those dunes," Sir Roger announced.

"Gracious me!" exclaimed Sylvester. "Is it alive?"

Sir Roger drew his sword. "My ancestors killed many terrible beasts. Now I, alone, will attack and slay this one. Wait here until I return victorious." He galloped over the sand dunes.

The remaining Crusaders climbed off their horses and walked around, stretching their muscles.

Sir Roger Charges

Bugs sidled up to Sylvester. "While Sir Roger's chasing mirages, let's watch for our chance to sneak away."

"But Bugs, they'll spot us if we take the horses, and it'll take us days to get back on foot!"

"Yeah, but at least we can't drown on the way."

From beyond the dunes echoed Sir Roger's battle cry. The other three knights looked expectantly in the direction of the cry.

"Now!" hissed Bugs. He and Sylvester dashed around a couple of

"Let's Sneak Away."

sand dunes and raced across the desert the way they had come.

From behind came the pounding of horses' hooves.

"Hide among those rocks!" cried Bugs.

Just then Sir Ed galloped over the rocks. The other two knights came up from behind.

"Outflanked!" groaned Bugs.

The knights surrounded them with drawn swords. "What's the big idea? Trying to mess up a good deal?" Sir Max demanded quite indignantly.

Surrounded

"Listen, fellas," said Bugs, "you still think this is some kind of stunt for movies or TV—"

The three men agreed.

"But it isn't!" declared Bugs. "Sir Roger thinks he really *is* a genuine Crusader living back in the thirteenth century."

Sir Don began to argue, but Bugs held up his hand. "Have you seen any cameras? Any directors? Any sound equipment?"

"They make that stuff real tiny nowadays, long-ears," said Sir Max. "It's easier to move around then."

A Heated Argument

"Our armor is probably bugged with all that gear," added Sir Ed.

"We don't need directors," said Sir Don. "They want us to just act natural."

Sir Ed lifted his sword menacingly. "You're not going to wreck our chances, rabbit!"

"Er ... couldn't you merely allow us to resign?" asked Sylvester, eyeing the sword's edge.

"Absolutely not!" said Sir Max. "It would ruin the whole program if you dropped out now."

"From now on," said Sir Ed, "we

A Menacing Sword

will be guarding you two day and night. Now, march back!"

When they neared the place where Sir Roger had left them, they could hear the Crusader shouting battle cries as blows rang from his sword. The din became more furious; then suddenly it broke off.

Sir Roger rode back over the dunes, sword raised triumphantly. "The serpent is dead! His black blood is oozing all over the sand!"

"Black blood!" exclaimed Bugs. "Y'mean this is for real?"

He and Sylvester looked at each

"The Serpent Is Dead!"

other and then dashed over the dunes.

They soon came to a long cylinder that stretched for miles in either direction. From a gap hacked in its side gushed a black substance.

"Sir Blow-his-horn has really done it this time!" cried Bugs. "He's broken open an oil pipeline!"

A Bad Break

CHAPTER 7

BATTLE OF THE OASIS

A jeep bearing two Isitsandian oil technicians bounced over the noon-hot desert sands.

"We've followed twenty-five miles of pipeline since dawn," complained Omar, "and we haven't yet found the break recorded by our instruments at the refinery!"

Searching for the Oil Leak

"Let's stop for lunch," suggested Selim. "There's an oasis where we can eat."

Omar turned the jeep toward the oasis, and soon they arrived at the palm trees.

"You set up the picnic while I report our location," said Selim. Through the walkie-talkie, he told his boss of their failure to find the pipeline break.

"It must be in the next thirty miles," squawked the instrument. "By then you'll meet up with the other team of searchers."

Reporting Their Location

Selim signed off. Then he took a
transistor radio over to the palms.
He and Omar listened to music
while they ate.

"We've never had a pipeline
break this big before," said Omar.

"The boss thinks it's sabotage,"
Selim said.

"It must be outsiders, then," con-
cluded Omar. "The local people have
never bothered the line before."

On the other side of a nearby
sand dune, Sir Max studied the oil
technicians relaxing in the oasis.
Then he worked his way down to

Sir Max Watches

his hidden horse, mounted, and swiftly rode back the way he had come that morning.

A few miles away, Bugs and Sylvester drooped in their saddles as Sir Roger's army straggled over the burning sands.

"If those old knights ran into this kind of heat," panted Bugs, "it's no wonder that they lost all seven Crusades."

"Ho!" cried Sir Roger. "Yonder comes my advance scout."

Sir Max reined to a halt. "Enemy scouts are at the next oasis!"

"Yonder Comes My Scout."

"If they're looking for trouble," said Sir Roger with relish, "we'll give them plenty. Forward, men!"

They kicked their horses into a gallop and went thundering over the dunes.

At the oasis, the technicians lay sleepily in the shade. "Omar," yawned Selim, "I hear rumbling."

"A wild herd running," muttered Omar. Suddenly he sat bolt upright and pointed. "L-Look—men in armor. A-Attacking on h-horses!"

"The saboteurs!" cried Selim.

The men ran to the jeep and

"The Saboteurs!"

roared away in a cloud of dust.

"Radio in a report fast!" Omar ordered.

Selim reached for the walkie-talkie.

The Crusaders swept into the oasis. "Stand and fight!" Sir Roger shouted at the departing jeep. "Hmm . . . the dust is in the way, but that looks like an odd beast they're riding."

"It's called a jeep, Your Honor," explained Sylvester.

"Jeep, eh?" said Sir Roger. "Does it eat as much as a camel?"

A Hasty Retreat

The knights took off their armor and splashed in the oasis pool.

Bugs bubbled happily in the water. "All I need now is an inner tube and a gallon of iced carrot juice."

"A tin of frosted sardines for me," sighed Sylvester.

After their swim, Sir Roger invited his men to go through the things the technicians had left behind in their haste. "Choose what you want from our loot," he said.

"Look, Bugs," exclaimed Sylvester. "A transistor radio!"

"A touch of civilization!" cried

A Refreshing Swim

Bugs. Eagerly he turned it on.

"... latest news," said the radio. "A guerrilla force has apparently crossed the border into Isitsand."

"Heavens," muttered Sylvester, "hope we don't run into *them!*"

"... raided several villages along the river," the radio continued. "Yesterday the guerrillas damaged an oil pipeline. Technicians searching for the leak were attacked an hour ago at a small oasis."

Bugs turned to Sylvester with a startled expression.

"Sufferin' succotash, Bugs!" said

Alarming News

Sylvester. "They mean us, don't they?"

The radio went on: "The Isitsand government has declared a national emergency. The army, supported by the air force, is rushing to the oil fields. The navy is deploying around the lake and up the river."

"C'mon, Sylvester. We gotta somehow shake Iron Britches out of his century!"

Together they ran to Sir Roger.

"Doc, call off the conquest! We're surrounded. No kidding!"

"How do you know?" asked Sir

"We're Surrounded."

Roger suspiciously.

"I heard about it on this." Bugs showed him the radio. "A coupla thousand armed guys are coming after us!"

". . . very heavy artillery and tanks . . ." the radio intoned.

"Sorcery! A devil's instrument!" Sir Roger knocked the radio out of Bugs's hand and stamped it to bits. "Luckily, I was able to save you from that witchcraft."

Bugs and Sylvester tried to tell the other knights about the radio report, but no one believed them.

Smashing the Radio

"Now it's every man for himself,"
Bugs told Sylvester.

That night, when everyone else
seemed to be sound asleep, Bugs
and Sylvester crept away from the
oasis to where the horses were kept.
Sylvester clanked occasionally
from the camera equipment hidden
under his armor.

"Halt!" cried Sir Don, springing
out of some bushes. "Aha! We
thought you might try deserting!"

"Have a heart, doc," Bugs said.
"That radio report was true!"

Caught in the Act

"Back you go," ordered Sir Don. He marched them to the oasis. "I will be on guard all night, so don't try this trick again. This acting assignment is the chance of a lifetime. I don't understand why you two want to blow it."

"What's that noise, Bugs?" asked Sylvester, staring up through the moonlight.

"It's a small airplane," said Bugs. "Probably an army scout—"

POOF! A brilliant pink flower burst overhead, lighting up the ground around them.

A Flare Lights the Ground

"Flares!" exclaimed Bugs.

WHOOM! An explosion kicked up the dirt near them.

"Grenades!" yelled Sylvester.

"Reveille, reveille!" shouted Bugs, running through the palms. "Get up, you guys! We're under attack! Run for shelter!"

"We're Under Attack!"

CHAPTER 8

MYSTERY WRECK

The explosion had awakened the others. "To arms!" shouted Sir Roger. Sir Ed and Sir Max cowered behind a palm tree.

POOF! Another flare burst over the oasis. WHOOM! A grenade tore up some thornbushes.

Sir Roger gaped skyward. "It's

"To Arms!"

a flying dragon! The Isitsandians
sent this beast against us!"

"Down, doc, down!" yelled Bugs
as another flare lit up the oasis.

The crusading army jumped for
safety. WHOOM!

Bugs and Sylvester huddled next
to some rocks. "That scout plane
can't do much damage if we stay
under cover," said Bugs.

"He can radio our position to the
nearest Isitsandian air force base,
chum," said Sylvester.

"Yeah, that's right," Bugs
agreed nervously.

Nervous Companions

POOF! WHOOM! A dirt shower punctuated the glare lighting up the empty oasis.

"Say, Bugs, nobody's in sight."

"Well, what are we waiting for?"

Together, Bugs and Sylvester crept out of the oasis. With the aerial attack covering any sounds, they untied two horses and led them along the shadows of a line of cliffs. As they mounted, they heard the scout plane fly away.

"He must've run out of grenades," said Bugs.

"Where're we headed, pal?"

A Chance to Escape

"Back to the ruined castle," Bugs replied. "If we cut straight across the desert, we can hit it by tomorrow morning. Then we can pick up the road to the nearest city."

With the moon lighting their way, Bugs and Sylvester galloped over the dunes for hour after hour. At last Bugs halted. "Let's catch a little shut-eye, Sylvester."

They hitched their horses under a nearby cliff and went to sleep.

At dawn, Bugs was awakened by Sylvester. "Get up, Bugs! That scout plane's landed near us!"

"Get Up, Bugs!"

"Huh?" Bugs sat up. "Where?"

"Behind those cliffs. He must've come down for a nap last night before we got here."

"If we can convince the pilot that we're friendly types," said Bugs hopefully, "it'll save us a long trip to town."

They tiptoed around the cliffs to a small plane resting on the sand.

"I don't see anybody around," said Bugs. "He must be inside the plane. Let's wake him slow and easy."

As they approached the craft,

Tiptoeing Toward the Plane

Bugs exclaimed, "Look, Sylvester, that wing's busted!"

"Sufferin' succotash, this plane crashed! But why didn't we hear the noise?"

"Hmm. Something's funny about this plane," said Bugs. "There's a lot of sand blown around it."

Sylvester marched up and put his head through an open window. "Sand's blown inside, too. Nothing else here, except a pile of papers."

"Let's take a gander, doc." Bugs reached through the window and pulled out some papers. "Letters,

Sylvester Looks Inside

a pilot's old logbook and— Gosh! Sylvester, this stuff's dated twenty-five years ago!"

"My word! Y'mean this plane's been here all that time?"

Going through the papers, Bugs and Sylvester pieced together the story of a foreign geologist working for the Isitsandian government. He flew a small airplane, searching for oil drilling sites. His wife and young son had been with him on this last trip when the plane crash-landed.

Sylvester sighed sadly. "Wonder

Bugs Reads the Log

what happened to the remains."

"Things just sorta blow away in the desert," said Bugs. "We oughta report this. Let's see— The family was named Smith, right?"

Sylvester read from a paper. "Smith. Jack, Lillian, and their son Roger."

"And their son Roger!" yelled Bugs, leaping into the air.

He came down running and zoomed straight up the side of the cliff. By the time Sylvester joined him, Bugs had proven his hunch.

"Look out there, old pal! What

Zooming up the Cliff

d'ya see on the horizon?"

"It—it's a castle, Bugs. Built into some distant cliffs."

"It's *the* castle, doc! Sir Roger's old hometown! D'ya get it now?"

"Sir Roger is young Roger Smith?" squeaked Sylvester. "The boy must've survived the plane crash!"

"Right! But he got hit on the head and wandered around in a daze, until he stumbled into that ruined castle. Sir Roger told us his earliest memory is of waking up in the ruins, with a terrific headache."

"It's *the* Castle!"

"Poor lad had amnesia," said Sylvester. "He'd forgotten his past."

"And growing up with those tapestries of knights and battles made him think he was a Crusader," added Bugs. "The few natives that strayed near the castle thought he was a ghost. Poor Sir Roger! Now he's got a modern army stacked against him."

"But, Bugs, those three other guys will surrender when they find out the bullets are real!"

"Sure they will," Bugs agreed.

"Poor Lad Has Amnesia."

"But Sir Roger will keep on fighting to the end—*his* end. That's the way they did it seven hundred years ago, and now he doesn't know any better."

"Bugs, we've got to save that poor man from himself!"

"Yeah," said Bugs. "But how?"

Imagining Sir Roger's Fate

CHAPTER 9

THE DRAGON'S LAIR

Hands clasped behind his back, Bugs walked in circles, thinking hard. His feet wore a rut in the dirt as his crafty rabbit brain invented and discarded plan after plan.

At last he snapped his fingers. "It just might work! Sylvester, let's see all that camera stuff you've been

Bugs Has an Idea

hauling around."

Sylvester untied the gear from various parts of himself. "It's all the latest stuff, Bugs. The camera doubles as a projector. This box develops the film. And—"

" 'Nuff said!" Bugs pushed Sylvester toward a small cave. "Here's your darkroom. Develop everything you've got! I'll tell you my plan while you work."

An hour later, Sylvester was finished. Mounting their horses, they rode away from the old plane wreck at a fast pace.

Galloping Off

Several hours later, Bugs rode back to the small oasis, hoping to pick up Sir Roger's trail as the Crusaders marched toward the distant oil field "fortress."

To Bugs's surprise, Sir Roger and the three knights were still at the oasis, busily strapping on their armor.

"Ho, Sir Bugs!" cried the last Crusader. "We were just setting out to look for you. We spent the whole morning capturing our horses. They were frightened away during last night's attack. Where

"Ho, Sir Bugs!"

is Sir Sylvester?"

"He—he's trapped, Sir Roger,"
moaned Bugs. "We must rescue him
at once!"

"Did the enemy capture him?"
asked Sir Don, putting on his
sword.

"No," Bugs said excitedly. "It
was the monster!"

"The flying dragon!" cried Sir
Roger. "I see what happened. As
you and Sir Sylvester slept, the
dragon stole forth and captured
him. Probably ate him up."

"No, he's still alive, trapped in

"It Was the Monster!"

the dragon's lair. Please hurry and save him, Sir Roger!"

"We'll rescue him as soon as we capture the great fortress," said Sir Roger.

"You'll need every man to take that fortress," argued Bugs. "And besides, the dragon might attack our flank."

"Wisely spoken, rabbit. Very well, lead me to the dragon's lair!"

As they rode out of the oasis, Sir Ed leaned close to Bugs. "What's the big idea?" he demanded in a low voice.

"What's the Big Idea?"

Sir Don, on the other side, added, "Why did you run off again and then come back alone?"

Bugs shrugged. "We finally found out how things really stand."

"Oh, I get it," said Sir Max. "You met the movie director! Now you know that this is a movie, just as we've been telling you all along."

"You're warm, doc," said Bugs. "And right now we're heading for the big scene. It's been changed from the fortress to the dragon's cave."

"What's that rumbling noise?"

"You Met the Movie Director!"

asked Sir Don. "Sounds like *tanks*."

"Uh . . . army maneuvers," said Bugs nervously. "That's why the scene was changed." He galloped up alongside Sir Roger. "Better hurry, doc. I don't know how long Sir Sylvester can hold out."

Spurring their horses, the party galloped to the cliffs and ravines, following Bugs. The distant rumbling noise was growing louder.

"Hear that?" Bugs asked Sir Roger. "The dragon's getting hungry! There's the cave where he took Sir Sylvester."

"Better Hurry, Doc!"

"Have courage, Sir Sylvester!" shouted the Crusader. He jumped off his horse, drew his sword, and charged into the cave. As soon as he was gone, Bugs turned to the three knights.

"Okay, you guys," he said, "this is the big scene. When the troops get here, you surrender without a fight. Then Sir Roger will come out of the cave and rescue you."

The knights nodded. Bugs said, "I'll go and give Sir Roger his cue." He dashed into the cave.

"This Is the Big Scene."

CHAPTER 10

A SHIFT IN TIME

Bugs blinked in the cave's darkness. "Yoo-hoo, Sir Roger!" he called. "Where are you?"

Far down one tunnel, he heard someone thrashing and thumping about. "Here, Sir Bugs! I can't find that dratted dragon!"

"Oops, he's in the wrong end,"

"Yoo-hoo, Sir Roger!"

Bugs muttered. He raced down the tunnel, stumbled, and heard a sword *swish* over his head. "T-Take it easy, your knightship—it's me! I'll lead you to the action."

Taking the Crusader by the arm, Bugs led him toward the other tunnel. As they passed by the cave's entrance, they heard the distant rumbling of the tanks. "Down here, sir," said Bugs, pushing Sir Roger ahead of him. "I'll show you."

Suddenly a big square of light shone on the cave wall. The first of Sylvester's movies flashed on. They

Swish!

were pictures of the people aboard the ocean liner on which Bugs and Sylvester had sailed to Isitsand.

Sir Roger stopped for a moment, then started toward the wall, sword uplifted.

"Hey," called Bugs, "where ya going, doc?"

"Down this tunnel," replied Sir Roger. "Those people all must have been captured by the dragon. I shall rescue them!"

"Wait a minute! That isn't a tunnel," Bugs explained. "They're just pictures—like a tapestry, sort of."

"Wait a Minute!"

"Pictures that move?" demanded Sir Roger. "The Isitsandian magicians must be casting a spell on us! I'll cut them to pieces!" Sir Roger began swinging his sword.

"Relax, doc," Bugs urged. "Enjoy the show."

Sir Roger grabbed Bugs by the ears. "Traitor!" he cried. "You're one of them!"

Bugs gulped. "Uh . . . look out, doc! There's the flying dragon!" He pointed toward the movies flashing on the wall. The scene was now the small Isitsandian airport that he

"Traitor!"

and Sylvester had visited. An airplane was coming in for a landing.

"Aha!" yelled Sir Roger.

"*Now*, Sylvester!" cried Bugs.

From his hiding place on the small ledge overhead, Sylvester dropped a large rock directly on top of Sir Roger's helmeted head. BONG!

The Crusader's grip on Bugs's ears loosened. Sir Roger stood very still for a moment, staring at the movie. Then, in a small voice, he said, "My daddy has a plane just like that one. He takes me flying

BONG!

with him all the time." He looked
around the cave. "I remember now!
We were flying, and we crashed.
I—I woke up in that old castle. My
head hurt." He dropped his sword.
"Why, I'm not a Crusader at all,
am I?"

Bugs shook his head. "Nope."

Roger Smith looked worried.
"And we're in b-big t-trouble?"

Bugs nodded. "Yep."

There was a commotion outside
the entrance to the cave. Suddenly
dozens of Isitsandian troups poured
into the underground room, their

"I Remember Now!"

weapons aimed at Bugs and Roger
Smith. The three ex-knights, Max,
Ed, and Don, with raised hands and
worried expressions, were led in by
rough-looking soldiers.

Then the short, fat Isitsandian
general shouldered his way through
the crowd. "You were wise to surrender without a fight," he said
gruffly. "I have the entire area surrounded with tanks." The general
leaned up close to Roger Smith and
sneered. "My government does not
take kindly to guerrilla raiders.
You will be spending many, many

Captured!

years in a damp, dark prison cell—"

"Perfect!" cried Sylvester from his perch atop the small ledge. "Hold that expression! Let me get a close-up."

There were surprised murmurings from the soldiers as Sylvester jumped down from the ledge, movie camera in hand. Very slowly, he advanced toward the general, camera whirring, until the lens was nearly touching the general's nose.

"Cut!" Sylvester shouted.

"What is the meaning of this?" growled the Isitsandian general.

"Hold That Expression!"

Sylvester studied the man's face, from one angle and then another. "Ah, such a face you've got, General! So expressive! When they see this in the States, you'll be a *star!*"

The general's expression softened. "Me—a star? You mean—"

"That's right, doc," Bugs interrupted. "We've been making a movie. And what a climax! You and your soldiers were terrific!"

Max and Ed and Don sighed loudly and lowered their arms. "I-I knew it all a-long," gulped Max. The others nodded weakly.

"Me—a Star?"

Bugs slapped the general on the back. "The cast party will be at the old castle tonight. You and your boys are all invited, of course. You will see yourselves performing."

The general beamed. The soldiers grinned and lowered their weapons.

"And then it's back to the States for us," Bugs continued. "No more Crusades. Right, Sir Roger?"

Roger Smith flushed. "Uh—just plain Roger is fine."

Bugs winked and shook hands with Roger. "The last Crusader," he added with a grin.

"No More Crusades."

Other BIG LITTLE BOOKS® Available

BATMAN—The Cheetah Caper

*****BUGS BUNNY**—The Last Crusader

*****DONALD DUCK**—The Lost Jungle City

THE FANTASTIC FOUR in the House of Horrors

GRIMM'S GHOST STORIES

LASSIE—Old One-Eye

THE LONE RANGER Outwits Crazy Cougar

MICKEY MOUSE—Mystery at Disneyland

*****THE PINK PANTHER**—Adventures in Z-Land

POPEYE—Danger, Ahoy!

SPIDER-MAN Zaps Mr. Zodiac

TWEETY AND SYLVESTER—The Magic Voice

*With "FLIP-IT" cartoons

WHITMAN® *Classics*

Books for Your Permanent Library

WHITMAN® *Mystery Adventures*

TRIXIE BELDEN